Olaf the Viking
The Dark Forest

Elizabeth Laird

Pictures by John Richardson

Collins

First published 1986 by William Collins Sons & Co Ltd, London and Glasgow
© text Elizabeth Laird 1986, © illustrations John Richardson 1986

Olaf the Viking
Is eight years old.
He is big and strong.
He is brave and bold.

Olaf's father
Is Bor the Wise.
Olaf's mother
Is Asta Bright-Eyes.

They live in a long house
Near the sea,
With sister Elma
And baby Loki.

The winter is long.
The winter is cold.
The cow's in the barn,
The sheep in the fold.

Asta the mother
Shakes her head.
She has no flour
To make her bread.

The store is empty,
There's nothing to eat.
The Vikings are hungry.
They want fresh meat.

Bor in his long house
Calls for his bow.
He will go hunting,
Out in the snow.

"Father," says Olaf,
"Let me come too.
  I can run fast,
  I can help you."

"Find your boots,
And find your spear.
Come with me, son,
To hunt the deer."

Olaf is happy,
He jumps for joy.
He's a hunter now,
A true Viking boy.

Into the forest
Dark and deep,
Bor and Olaf
Silently creep.

Marks of a deer
Are there in the snow.
Bor puts an arrow
Into his bow.

"What's that moving
  Over there?
  Help me! Father!
  It's a bear!"

The bear comes on
With a grunt and a crash.
Teeth that snap!
Eyes that flash!

Olaf is frightened,
But Bor stands still.
He shoots his arrow.
He makes his kill.

The bear falls dead
With a choking sound,
But Bor is under him
On the ground.

His eyes are shut.
His face is white.
Help must be found,
Before the night.

In the forest
Dark and deep,
Bears hunt,
Hares sleep.

In the trees
A wolf is howling.
Near his den
A fox is prowling.

Olaf is frightened,
But he runs fast.
He comes to the long house,
Home at last!

"Mother! Mother!
Call the men,
To bring my father
Home again!"

"Erik! Rigg!"
  The women shout.
"Harald! Har!
  Come out! Come out!"

The men come out
In the cold, cold night.
They run to the forest
In the dim moonlight.

Olaf and Asta
Wait in the hall.
"Bor's safe! All's well!"
They hear the men call.

The Vikings are feasting
All night long.
They eat and drink
And they sing this song:

"Olaf the Viking
   Is eight years old!
   He is big and strong!
   He is brave and bold!"